For Lauren, Dara, Walter, Osker and Markley

First published in Great Britain 2022 by Farshore

An imprint of HarperCollins*Publishers*
1 London Bridge Street, London SE1 9GF
www.farshorebooks.com

HarperCollins*Publishers*
1st Floor, Watermarque Building, Ringsend Road
Dublin 4, Ireland

Copyright © Alex Willmore 2022
Alex Willmore has asserted his moral rights.

ISBN 978 0 00856 109 3 (HB)
ISBN 978 0 00850 357 4 (PB)
Printed in Italy
001

A CIP catalogue record for this title is available from the British Library.

Stay safe online. Farshore is not responsible for content hosted by third parties.

Farshore takes its responsibility to the planet and its inhabitants very seriously.
We aim to use papers from well-managed forests run by responsible suppliers.

I DID SEE A MAMMOTH!

ALEX WILLMORE

Farshore

We're exploring the Antarctic for penguins.
But I'm going to see a MAMMOTH.

Don't be silly! You can't see a mammoth! And why would you want to when you can see . . .

FABULOUS,

CUTE,

GLORIOUS,

PENGUINS!

But I'm not here to see penguins . . .

I'm here to see a mammoth.

I'm *going* to see a . . .

MAMMOTH! MAMMOTH! MAMMOTH! MAMMOTH! MAMMOTH!

LOOK! I saw a great big mammoth,
on a skateboard . . .
wearing SUNGLASSES!

Er, you can't have seen a mammoth.
Mammoths are extinct. And I'm pretty
sure they're not even from around here.

Are you certain what you saw wasn't
a wonderful, majestic, glorious penguin . . .
on a skateboard . . . wearing sunglasses?

It *wasn't* a silly penguin.
I didn't see a penguin.

I definitely, definitely, definitely saw a . . .

M. . M. . . M. . . .

MAMMOTH!

I saw a mammoth!
A great big mammoth
on a skateboard,
wearing sunglasses
and a tutu
and doing BALLET!

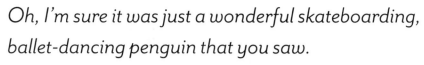

Oh, I'm sure it was just a wonderful skateboarding, ballet-dancing penguin that you saw.

Pfft.

I *did* see a mammoth.

I absolutely,
definitely saw a . . .

MAMMOTH! MAMMOTH!

MAMMOTH! MAMMOTH!

I SAW A GREAT BIG MAMMOTH

on a SKATEBOARD,

wearing SUNGLASSES

and a TUTU and a TOP HAT

and also it was SWIMMING

using FLIPPERS . . .

AND A SNORKEL!

No . . .

you . . .

didn't!

Yes. I. DID.

I'll show you.

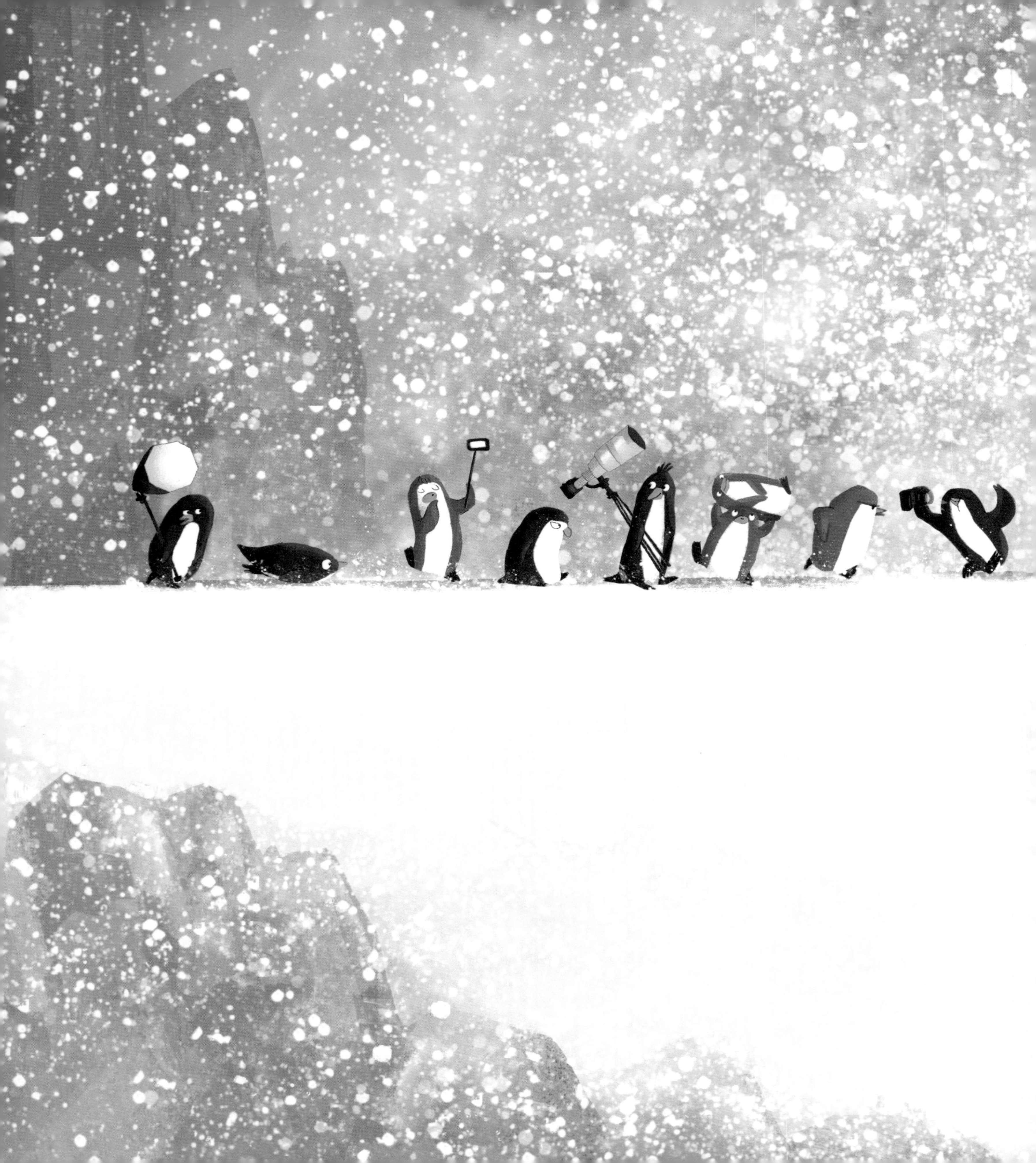

It's right over . . .

. . . here?!

NO!
NO!
NO!
NO!

I DID SEE A

M·A·M

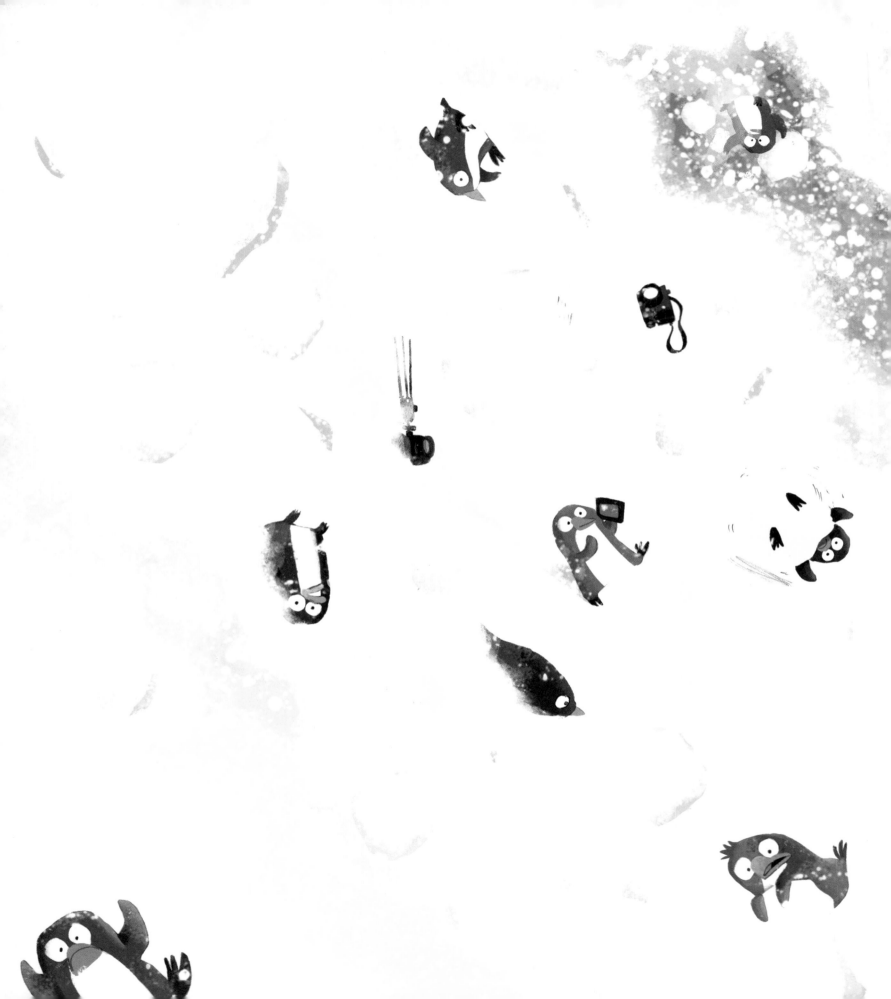

Sigh. Maybe I *didn't* see a . . .

MAMMOTH!!!

Woolly mammoths are ancient relatives of today's elephants. If you'd been alive 10,000 years ago, and lived in northern Europe, northern Asia, north America or the Arctic, you might well have met one.

Meeting a penguin is a lot easier. The southern hemisphere is home to eighteen different species, including five species that live in Antarctica. So far, no evidence of mammoths has been found there - but there's no harm looking!